Magnificent
MABEL
and the Magic Caterpillar

Ruth
Quayle

Julia
Christians

First published in the UK in 2021 by Nosy Crow Ltd
The Crow's Nest, 14 Baden Place,
Crosby Row, London SE1 1YW

www.nosycrow.com

ISBN: 978 1 78800 596 8

A CIP catalogue record for this book is available from the British Library.

Printed and bound in the UK by Clays Ltd, Elcograf S.p.A.

Papers used by Nosy Crow are made from wood grown in sustainable forests.
1 3 5 7 9 10 8 6 4 2

www.nosycrow.com

1

Magnificent Mabel
and the
Magic Caterpillar

In our class at school we have two teachers and one white board and we have twenty-eight children.

We also have a class caterpillar whose name is Steve.

Every night, somebody has a turn taking Steve home and looking after him.

All the other children have had their turn, especially Torin Ray, who had three turns because he was allowed to look after Steve for the whole weekend.

Torin Ray lives next door to our teacher, Mr Messenger.

Torin Ray is always being lucky.

Every afternoon I jump up and down on the carpet and stick my hand in the air. I call out in my loud, persuading voice and I say, "Please can I look after Steve this evening, Mr Messenger?"

But Mr Messenger always picks someone who is sitting

nicely on their spot and who isn't
calling out.

This is the whole tragedy of
my life.

Mum says my turn will come and that I have to be patient and not call out. Dad tells me not to worry because caterpillars are not very interesting to look after anyway. But Dad does not know Steve.

Nobody does.

If they did they would know that Steve is an unusual caterpillar with magic powers.

Steve only shows these magic
powers to certain special people,
and I am very lucky because
one of these special people is me,
Mabel Chase.

I am actually Steve's special person in true life.

When everyone else in the class had already had a go at looking after Steve, I thought that this Wednesday it was going to be my turn.

In the morning before school on Wednesday, I gobbled up my breakfast.

I got dressed in a jiffy.

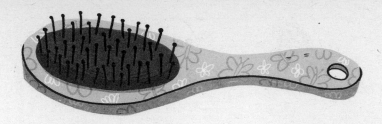

I let my sister Meg borrow my best hair band and I didn't even make her give me one of her things in return.

I brushed my teeth for two whole minutes with the minty toothpaste which I do not like as much as the bubblegum one that Mum only lets me use at Christmastime.

I didn't moan about itchy legs or hurty hair.

I didn't say, "that's not fair", not even once.

Dad said, "Blimey, what's got into Mabel?"

Mum said, "Whatever it is, I hope it lasts."

But I couldn't even hear them properly.

I was busy thinking. When I

think my brain gets very busy.

I was planning what Steve and I were going to do together later after school.

I thought, Steve and I could cuddle up together in bed and have a midnight feast.

I thought, Steve could take me to Caterpillar Land to visit the other magic caterpillars.

I thought, Steve and I will go on a special adventure.

All day long at school, I kept catching Steve's eye and winking at him.

I knew that Steve could understand my winks because Steve is magic and I am a bit too. At break time, I stayed inside on my own so I could chat to Steve.

When Edward Silitoe saw me, he laughed and pointed and said I was a mad girl. But I didn't even poke Edward Silitoe in the tummy. I just felt sorry for Edward Silitoe because he didn't know that Steve was a magic caterpillar.

At home time when we were getting our coats

and lunch boxes, Mr Messenger
picked up Steve's container.

He said, "Who hasn't had a
go at taking Steve home yet?"

I jumped up and down all
wriggly and I put my hand up. I
tried not to shout out but a bit of
a shout came out anyway.

Luckily I didn't have to worry
because mine was the only hand
up.

Mr Messenger smiled and
said, "Then it must be your turn,
Mabel. I'm sure you will look
after Steve very well because I
believe you are extremely keen
on pets."

I thought it was very nice of
Mr Messenger to know that I am
keen on pets so I gave him my
best smile.

I said, "That's true, Mr

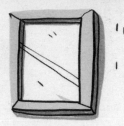

Messenger. I have a knack with caterpillars."

And then I said very quietly so that nobody could hear me, "Especially magic ones."

Mr Messenger handed Steve's box to me and I carefully carried Steve all the way home without asking for any help.

I put Steve's box in a cool, dark spot in my bedroom

because I didn't want Steve to
get sunburnt.

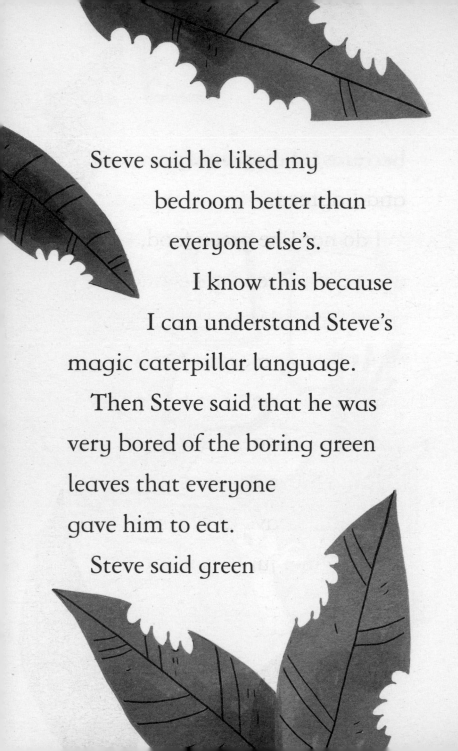

Steve said he liked my
bedroom better than
everyone else's.
I know this because
I can understand Steve's
magic caterpillar language.
Then Steve said that he was
very bored of the boring green
leaves that everyone
gave him to eat.
Steve said green

leaves were disgusting,
and I agreed.

I do not like green food,
except for green sweets and
green ice lollies and the crisps
that come in a green packet.

Steve told me that he prefers
pink food to eat.

I told Steve not to worry.

I said, "Leave it to Mabel
Chase, chief jungle explorer."

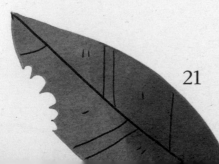

Then I packed a rucksack and
some water and a few emergency
supplies such as a torch and a
smallish biscuit, and I set off to
the jungle to find food for Steve.

This took a long time because
I had to hide from tigers and
snakes.

I had to cross a swamp full of crocodiles.

I had to swing through winding branches.

Luckily I found some juicy
pink food for Steve
at the top of
a very tall
tree.
Then I
trekked all
the way home.
Mum said I had to wash my
hands and eat my dinner before
I gave Steve his pink food.

She also said there was ice cream for pudding, which is not an everyday thing, so I did not like to argue with her.

After fish fingers and ice cream, Mum said I was allowed to go up to feed Steve his pink food.

But I happened to notice that the pink food I had picked had got all squishy — so I had to go

all the way back to the jungle to pick some more.

It was a long way back to the jungle and I got very dirty.

So then I had to spend a long time washing myself in the Amazon.

And after that I had to climb the world's tallest mountain to get back to Steve.

I thought, being a jungle explorer is very tiring and I am actually quite worn out.

I thought, I'll just have a little lie-down before taking Steve to Caterpillar Land with me.

I told Steve to wake me up for our midnight feast but I

don't think he heard me because
when I woke up it was already
morning.

I said, "Good morning, Steve."
But then I got a shock.
Because when I looked in
Steve's container ...

... there was no Steve.

All I could see was small
leaves and medium-sized leaves
and one extra-large great fat
green leaf hanging in the middle
of the branch.

I thought, I hope I didn't leave
Steve's container open last night.

When Meg came in to say
good morning, I did not say
good morning back.

I pointed to Steve's cage.

Meg looked for a long time then she made a gaspy sound.

Meg said, "Oh, Mabel!"

Meg said, "You've lost Steve."

I looked at Meg and made my eyes go straight.

I did not say one single word.

I thought, my sister is such a fusspot.

Meg patted me on the arm. She said, "Don't cry, Mabel. I'm

sure it's not your fault."

I said, "Meg, if you think I'm crying you are wrong."

I said, "There is nothing to cry about."

I said, "Steve is not lost. Steve is right there. Look."

I pointed at Steve's cage.

Meg shook her head.

She said, "Steve is not there, Mabel. Steve has gone."

I made my eyes even straighter. I said, "You can't see Steve because Steve has made himself invisible. Steve is a magic caterpillar and I am the only person who can see him."

Meg looked a bit panicky.

"Mabel," she said. "What are you going to say to Mr Messenger?"

I did not want to speak to Meg.

Meg was not being kind to me.

I went downstairs.

At breakfast I wasn't hungry.

My tummy hurt quite a lot.

I thought, I am ill and I should not be going to school today.

But my mum is not very good at telling when I am ill.

Mum said I had to go to school.

So I went.

I carried invisible, magic Steve all the way there.

I talked to him and I sang quietly.

Meg looked at me with a worried face.

Meg said, "Mabel, do you want me to come and see Mr Messenger with you?"

I said, "No thank you, Meg" and waved goodbye.

I took Steve straight to my classroom.

My tummy felt VERY hurty now.

I thought, I am not a well girl.

I thought, Mum should NOT

have sent me to school.

In the classroom, Edward Silitoe looked in Steve's container.

He stared for a long time. Then he said, "Mabel Chase has lost Steve."

Other children came over and shook their heads.

Elsa Kavinsky said, "It is a bad crime to lose our class caterpillar."

Matthew Juniper said, "You will be sent to the head and you might go to prison."

I ignored Edward Silitoe and I ignored

Elsa Kavinsky and I ignored
Matthew Juniper too.

I ignored all the other children
who were whispering about me.

I winked at invisible Steve and
he winked back.

At register, I took Steve up to
Mr Messenger.

My tummy was hurtier than
ever now.

Mr Messenger said, "Well,

Mabel, did you enjoy looking after Steve?"

I did not look at Mr Messenger.

I stared at the wall.

Edward Silitoe said, "Mabel Chase has lost our class caterpillar. Mabel Chase has lost Steve."

Mr Messenger peered into Steve's cage.

I gave Edward Silitoe my look that I give to people when I don't like them very much.

I said, "I have not lost Steve."

I said, "Steve is right there."

I said, "Steve is a magic caterpillar. Steve is invisible."

Everybody chattered and whispered and wriggled.

Everybody laughed about me, Mabel Chase.

I thought, it's time my mum came and picked me up.

I thought, I am not a well child.

Mr Messenger looked at me and smiled.

Mr Messenger said, "Congratulations, Mabel, you are quite right."

He said, "Steve IS there and he HAS made himself invisible."

Mr Messenger pointed at the
big, fat green leaf hanging on a
branch in Steve's container.

The other children stared and
I couldn't help staring too.

Mr Messenger told us that

Steve had wrapped himself up in
a thing called a chrysalis.

Mr Messenger said that when
Steve was ready to come out of
his chrysalis he would turn into
a beautiful butterfly.

Mr Messenger said, "It's sort of magic", and he smiled at me.

I looked at Mr Messenger carefully to check he wasn't teasing us because I am not keen on being teased one bit.

Teasing is worse than pinching.

But Mr Messenger said he wasn't teasing. He said he was telling the truth and then he got

48

out an actual published book
with real pictures to show us.

Everybody jumped up and
down. They shouted out in loud
voices. They stuck their hands in
the air. Mr Messenger had to tell
everybody to pipe down so he
could do the register.

But I did not jump up and
down and I didn't shout out
either.

I sat very still and I kept an
eye on Steve.

I gave him my special wink.

I whispered to him.

I said, "I knew you were
magic. I just knew it."

2

Magnificent Mabel
and the
Disappearing
Homework

On Fridays my sister Meg gets
homework.

I do not get homework.

I have to wait until I am older.

When Mum and Dad help
Meg with her homework I have
to play quietly on my own.

Playing quietly is harder than
doing homework.

Anyone can see I am the left-
out one in this family.

Sometimes on
Fridays Meg's
friend Max Roberts
comes over after
school and they do their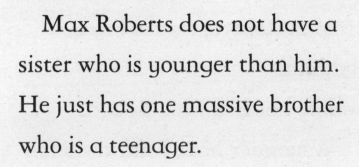
homework together.

Max Roberts does not have a
sister who is younger than him.
He just has one massive brother
who is a teenager.

Max Roberts is a know-it-all.

He says to Meg, "Your sister is out of control."

He says, "You should be stricter with your sister."

He says, "Your sister is starting to show off."

Max Roberts thinks I'm a handful.

I do not like Max Roberts.

Whenever Max Roberts comes to play or do homework, I invite

my friend Marcella round to
keep me company.

The thing about Marcella is
that she is very quiet.

She is so quiet that she hides
from most people.

Marcella won't let anyone see
her except for me.

Marcella is kind.

Marcella doesn't like it when I
get left out.

When Max Roberts said I
wasn't allowed to join in with
making a den with him and
Meg, Marcella waited until they
weren't looking, then she kicked
down their den.

And when we were making
necklaces and Max Roberts
wouldn't let me have any of the
pink beads Marcella waited till

Max Roberts went to the toilet
then she pushed Max Roberts's
necklace on the floor and his
pink beads spilt everywhere.

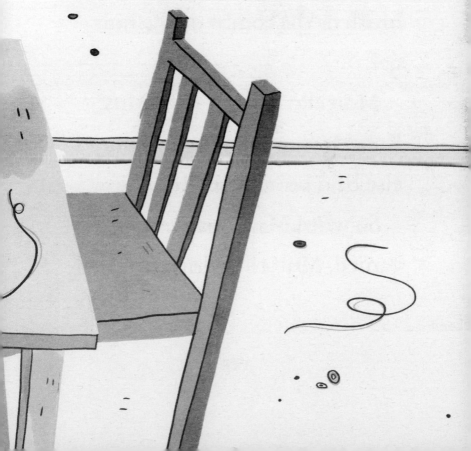

And when Max Roberts and
Meg were playing hairdressers,
Marcella spotted that Max
Roberts was not sharing the
brush or the combs or the hair
gel.

Marcella noticed that Max
Roberts would not let anyone
else be a hairdresser.

So when Max's back was
turned, Marcella got some

scissors from the kitchen and
she cut off a large chunk of Max
Roberts's black hair.

This made Max Roberts mad.

Max Roberts thought it was me who had cut off his hair.

Max Roberts told my mum.

When Max Roberts's mum came to collect him, Max Roberts told her too.

Max Roberts's mum said "Gosh" in a shocked voice.

My mum said "Sorry" and looked all fidgety.

I couldn't say it was Marcella and not me because Marcella is a secret person who doesn't like people seeing her.

Also, Marcella is my good friend.

Now when Max Roberts

comes over on Fridays to do homework with Meg my mum hides the scissors.

Mum also tries to keep me out of their way.

She says Max Roberts and Meg are older than me and I should leave them by themselves on their own.

But my problem is, Marcella won't leave them alone.

Marcella does not trust Max Roberts one inchy bit.

That's because Max Roberts is too neat.

He has clean shoes and white socks and he also has smart jumpers that are bought just for him and not handed down from cousins or sisters.

When he eats he doesn't dribble or spill or knock over his glass.

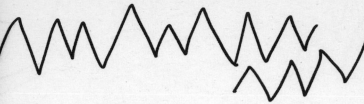

Max Roberts has very tidy
handwriting.

When Max Roberts came last
Friday, he said, "Let's do our
homework."

"OK," said Meg, even though
I could tell she didn't want to do
her homework one bit.

I said, "I'd better do my
homework too", and I sighed
like Dad does when he has lots

of work to do.

Max Roberts laughed at me
and he whispered to Meg.

He said, "Your sister can't even
write."

So I gave Max Roberts a mean
look and I showed him my best
squiggles.

Max Roberts did not notice
my mean look and he laughed
at my squiggles.

67

For their homework, Max Roberts and Meg had to write about their favourite lunch.

Meg wrote about fish fingers and chips because that's her most delicious thing to eat in the universe.

But Max Roberts said, "I'm going to write about slow-cooked lamb and rosemary potatoes."

Max Roberts eats a lot of interesting food because he goes to grown-up restaurants with his mum and dad.

Max Roberts says this is why he has such good table manners.

I kept an eye on Max Roberts
when he did his homework.

Max Roberts did not like this.

He said, "I don't like you
watching me."

He said, "You're putting me
off."

Meg said sorry to Max
Roberts but she couldn't
do anything
because in our

house watching someone is not actually doing anything wrong.

I watched Max Roberts write ten whole lines and fill one page of his homework with no rubbings-out.

Max Roberts's writing was joined up and lovely.

When Max Roberts had finished, he looked at Meg's homework which was not as neat as his and he said, "Well done, Meg", just like a grown-up.

This made me feel quite cross and boily.

I said, "Meg's is gooder."

But Meg said, "Don't be silly, Mabel. Max's writing is much better than mine."

And Max Roberts said, "Never mind, it's not a competition, is

it?"

So I said, "What's so special about homework anyway?"

Meg and Max Roberts didn't answer. They went upstairs to play schools.

I thought, I won't follow them.

I thought, I will stay here and keep Marcella company.

Marcella and I were very quiet and sensible.

We didn't go upstairs and disturb Meg and Max Roberts.

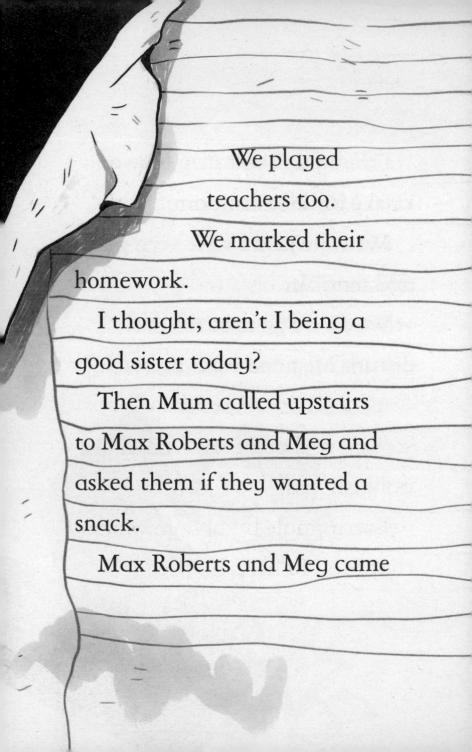

We played
teachers too.
We marked their
homework.
I thought, aren't I being a
good sister today?
Then Mum called upstairs
to Max Roberts and Meg and
asked them if they wanted a
snack.
Max Roberts and Meg came

racing down the stairs and sat
at the table next to me.

We were just
finishing our biscuits
when Max Roberts
opened his homework book.

Max Roberts started to
scream and yell and make a big
babyish fuss.

Every single bit of homework
that Max Roberts had spent

so long doing had been rubbed out, and it had been rubbed out so strongly the pages were all wrinkly and smudgy.

I thought, Marcella is a very naughty girl.

I thought, wait till I get my hands on Marcella.

Max Roberts made his eyes go all glary. He glared at me all through supper and he was still

glaring when his mum came to
collect him.

"I must say, I'm shocked,"
said Max Roberts's mum.

"I know," said my mum, but
she didn't look shocked. She
looked tired.

Then my mum sent me up to
my bedroom.

A long time later when
Marcella had gone again and

I was feeling a bit lonely, Meg
came up to see me.

She was holding her
homework book in her hand.

"Mabel," said Meg. "How
come my homework isn't rubbed
out too?"

I looked at Meg's homework
with my thinking face.

I scrunched up my eyes.

I said, "Hmmmmm."

I said, "Maybe Marcella
thought your homework was
better."

And then I
gave Meg a
big hug.

3

Magnificent Mabel
and the
Eye Test

Sophie Simpson wears glasses and Sophie Simpson's glasses come in their very own red case.

That red glasses case opens slowly when you press a button and goes clickety-click when you close it.

Sophie Simpson is always clicking that case.

Sophie Simpson clicks that case whenever I am close by.

This is quite boasty of Sophie
Simpson because I need glasses
and a clickety case too.

$$\sqrt{xy^2} = Z$$

$$\overset{\circ}{x} \times x = C$$

$$x^2 - 3^2 - 4^2 = 0$$

$$(a^2+b^2) = (a-b)(a+b)$$

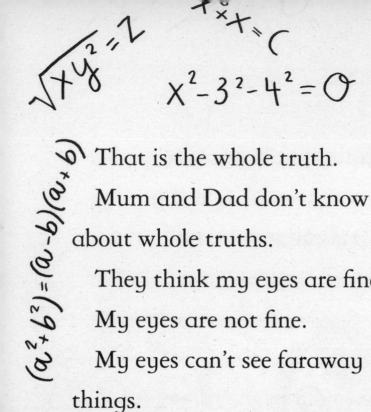

That is the whole truth.

Mum and Dad don't know about whole truths.

They think my eyes are fine.

My eyes are not fine.

My eyes can't see faraway things.

I can't see America from my bedroom.

$2/3$ x^2 $-\sqrt{x}$ $x^{3/\sqrt{x}}$ $= 0$

I can't spot a shooting
star in the dark night sky.

At school, maths is all muddly.

THAT is why I need glasses
that come with their own case.

When I explain this to my
mum and dad they smile and
shrug their shoulders.

Shrugging shoulders is a rude
thing to do.

Smiling breaks my feelings.

$$g(x) = \sqrt{x(x-a)(x-b)}$$

$$\frac{x^2 + y^2}{a^2} + \frac{z^2}{b^2} = 7$$

When I tell my teacher Mr
Messenger that maths is muddly
because I need glasses, Mr
Messenger tells me to move to
the front of the class to sit next
to Edward Silitoe.

Edward Silitoe is always
getting the right answers.

Edward Silitoe says if I
concentrate more I will be able
to see the maths just fine.

Sitting next to Edward Silitoe breaks my feelings too.

But even Edward Silitoe is not right about everything, because maths is muddly at the front of the class too.

Maths is muddly wherever I sit. That is not even a lie.

Maths is not muddly for Sophie Simpson and that is because Sophie Simpson has glasses.

If I had glasses and a clickety case like Sophie Simpson I would be able to see America and shooting stars and I would be able to see maths too.

I would be able to see as clear as crystal.

This is why I really, REALLY need glasses and a clickety case.

This is the whole tragedy of my life.

At break time on Friday, I asked Sophie Simpson if I could have a go with her glasses case but Sophie Simpson said, "No." Sophie Simpson said I might break her glasses case.

This made feel a bit hot and stampy and it also made me slightly push Sophie Simpson's glasses case out of her hand with my elbow accidentally.

Sophie Simpson told Mrs
Beaumont who was on
playground duty that I had
done this ON PURPOSE which

shows that Sophie Simpson does
not know about whole truths
either.

I had to have a little chat with
Mrs Beaumont and this made
me even more stampy because
I am not keen on chatting with
teachers.

Chatting with teachers is
another thing that breaks my
feelings.

That night, when I got home, my mum asked me what Mrs Beaumont had chatted to me about. I told her about Sophie Simpson not letting me use her glasses case. I explained that knocking the glasses case out of her hand was an accident. I said this was the whole truth.

My mum sighed and closed her eyes.

My mum is always closing her eyes.

This is why she can't see the whole truth about me needing glasses.

"Mabel," said Mum. "Tomorrow I am taking you to the optician to get your eyes tested and then you will know for sure that you do not need glasses."

I thought, that's what SHE
thinks.

I thought, the optician will
tell my mum that
I cannot see
faraway things
like America
and shooting
stars and
maths and
then I will

have a pair of glasses and a
clickety case all of my own.

I thought, good.

I thought, I can't wait to click
my glasses case when Sophie
Simpson is near me.

On Saturday Dad stayed at
home to make our lunch and
Mum took me and my sister
Meg to the optician's.

Meg did not need her eyes

tested because
she has had them
tested before but
she came to give me
moral support.

I thought that was quite bossy
of Meg.

At the opticians, the waiting
room was very quiet and my
mum and Meg got out their
books. Meg let me sit next to her

while she was reading so I could
look at the pictures.

But I could not see the pictures
because, remember, my eyes
were all muddly.

I had to hum instead.

"Mabel," whispered Meg. "In
waiting rooms you are meant
to sit quietly and look
at books. You are not
supposed to hum."

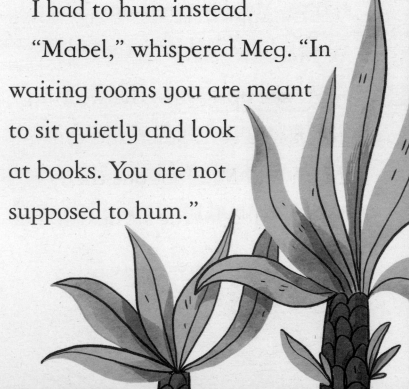

I gave Meg my nicest expression.

"Meg," I said patiently. "When you have muddly eyes you can't read books in waiting rooms. You have to hum. That is why I need glasses and a clickety case."

Meg smiled at Mum and Mum winked at Meg.

But instead of getting hot and

stampy and poking Meg a teeny bit hard in the tummy, I smiled too.

Because I was feeling so happy about getting glasses and a clickety case all of my own.

Eventually, after a long time, when I was starting to get bored of humming, the optician came out from behind a door and said, "Mabel Chase?"

And I stood up because Mabel
Chase is my whole name.

Mum, Meg and I followed the
optician into a small dark room.
Along one wall was a shelf full of
glasses and glasses cases.

The optician told me his name
was Sandeep Roy. Then he said,
"What is the problem?"

I told Sandeep Roy that I
couldn't see America from my

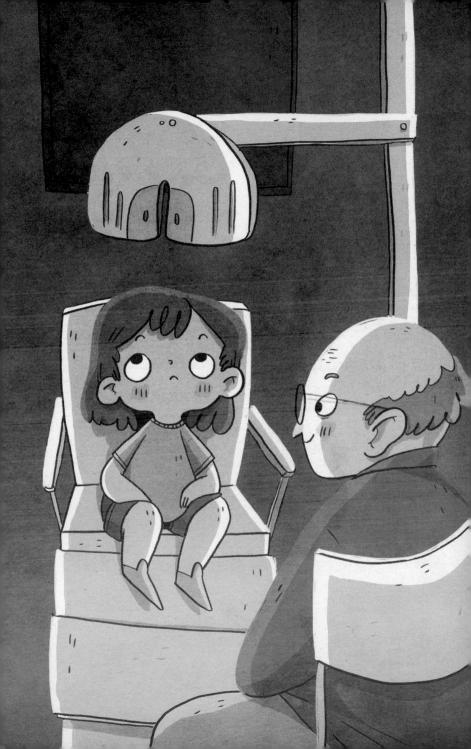

bedroom and I couldn't spot a
shooting star.

I told him that maths was
muddly even at the front of the
class next to Edward Silitoe.

I told him I needed glasses and
I especially needed a clickety
case because Sophie Simpson has
one and she doesn't find maths
muddly.

Sandeep Roy smiled and said,

"Well, Mabel, I'd better have an extra-good look at your eyes then."

I thought, I am glad that Sandeep Roy is a kind and pleasant person.

I thought, I am glad that SOMEONE is finally seeing the whole truth about me needing glasses and a case that goes clickety-click.

Sandeep Roy showed me some tiny letters and some teeny pictures.

He pointed to a capital T and said, "I don't suppose you can you tell me what this letter is?"

I scrunched up my eyes and said, "No. That capital T is VERY muddly."

Sandeep Roy smiled. He pointed

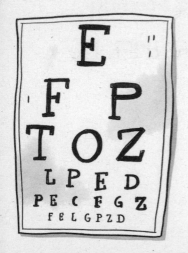

106

to a teeny cat and said, "What about this one?"

I said, "I'm sorry to break your feelings but that cat is muddly too."

After that Sandeep Roy spent a long time peering into my eyes with a small telescope.

He said "Hmmmm" a lot. He said, "Ah."

I thought, my muddly eyes must be very fascinating.

While Sandeep Roy was examining my eyes, I tried to have a good look at all the glasses on the shelf.

I spotted a round purple pair and I also saw a silver case that looked like it might go clickety-click.

I thought, those are the ones

I'm going to choose.

I thought, I can't wait.

After a long time, Sandeep
Roy stopped looking at my eyes
and stood up straight.

"I must say," he said. "It's
a shame that your eyes are so
muddly."

"Yes," I said. "Life is quite
tricky for me, Mabel Chase."

Sandeep smiled again. He was
a very smiley optician.

"If only you didn't have such

muddly eyes," he said, "you could have helped me find some missing treasure. Earlier today, I dropped a rare and valuable gold ring somewhere on the carpet but, because it is so tiny, only someone with very good eyesight will be able to spot it."

I nodded again.

I thought, that IS a shame.

I thought, I am good at

finding things that are lost.

I thought, I like things that
are rare and valuable.

I thought, I AM MABEL
CHASE, TREASURE
HUNTER.

Mum got up from her chair and started peering all squintily at the carpet.

Then Meg got down on her hands and knees and started to hunt in the dusty corners of the room.

I looked at Mum and Meg and I thought, those two will never find that rare and valuable treasure because they are not treasure hunters.

I thought, those two need my help.

So I tried my best not to think about my poor muddly eyes and I set off to search for the treasure.

I dug holes in the sand.

I hunted in
caves.

I fought off
giant bats.

Until eventually I spotted a teeny sparkly gold ring behind a thick palm tree.

"I've found it!" I said. "I've found the missing treasure!"

I handed that rare and valuable ring to Sandeep Roy.

Sandeep Roy smiled more than ever.

"Thank goodness," he said. "None of my other patients have been able to find my ring – their eyes are too muddly. Mabel, your eyes are magnificent."

I looked at Mum and Meg and they were smiling too.

"Well," I said. "I AM a treasure hunter."

"Ah, that explains it," said Sandeep Roy. "I've always noticed that treasure hunters have the best eyesight in the business. Treasure hunters never need to wear glasses."

I thought, oh.

I thought, but I really want those purple glasses and the silver clickety case.

I thought, now Sandeep Roy

has broken my feelings.

I stared at my shoe and I bit my lip.

"What treasure hunters DO need," said Sandeep Roy, "is something to put their tiny bits of treasure in."

Sandeep Roy walked across the room towards the shelf.

I looked up.

Sandeep Roy picked up the

silver glasses case and then
Sandeep Roy walked back across
the room and handed that silver
glasses case to me, Mabel Chase.

"A treasure hunter like you
is going to need a treasure box.
Am I right?"

I stroked the silver case. It was
smooth and shiny and it didn't
have one single scratch or dent.

I said "Yes" in a tiny voice.

And then I said "Thank you" a bit louder.

On the way home, I held my silver case very carefully because I didn't want it to get scratched or dented.

When I pushed the button it opened slowly.

When I closed it, it went clickety-click.

At break time on Monday, I

took my treasure box into the playground to look for treasure.

I was just looking for treasure in a swamp full of crocodiles when Sophie Simpson walked over.

Sophie Simpson said, "Mabel, why have you got a glasses case when you don't even need to wear glasses?"

And I said, "Sophie Simpson,

if you think this is a glasses case then you are wrong. This is not a glasses case, this is a treasure box, and I need it because I am a treasure hunter."

Sophie Simpson stared at my glasses case.

Sophie Simpson said, "How did you get to be a treasure hunter?"

And I said, "It's because I have the best eyes in the business. I can see America from my bedroom and I am good at spotting shooting stars. I still find maths muddly but that doesn't matter because if you're a treasure hunter you don't have to worry about things like maths."

"Mabel," said Sophie Simpson. "Are you fibbing?"

"No, Sophie Simpson," I said. "I'm not fibbing. That is the whole truth."